E
Tus

Tusa, Tricia.
Maebelle's suitcase

PERMA-BOUND.

DATE DUE			

Tricia Tusa
MAEBELLE'S SUITCASE

Aladdin Books
Macmillan Publishing Company New York
Collier Macmillan Canada Toronto
Maxwell Macmillan International Publishing Group
New York   Oxford   Singapore   Sydney

First Aladdin Books edition 1991
Aladdin Books
Macmillan Publishing Company
866 Third Avenue
New York, NY 10022
Collier Macmillan Canada, Inc.
1200 Eglinton Avenue East
Suite 200
Don Mills, Ontario M3C 3N1
Printed in the United States of America
A hardcover edition of *Maebelle's Suitcase* is available
from Macmillan Publishing Company.
2 3 4 5 6 7 8 9 10
Tusa, Tricia.
Maebelle's suitcase / Tricia Tusa. – 1st Aladdin Books ed.
p.   cm.
Summary: An elderly woman sacrifices a treasured prize to help her
friend, a young bird, make his first flight south.
ISBN 0-689-71444-0
[1. Old age – Fiction. 2. Friendship – Fiction. 3. Birds – Fiction.
4. Afro-Americans – Fiction.] I. Title.
[PZ7.T8825Mae 1991]
[E] – dc20   90–40678   CIP   AC

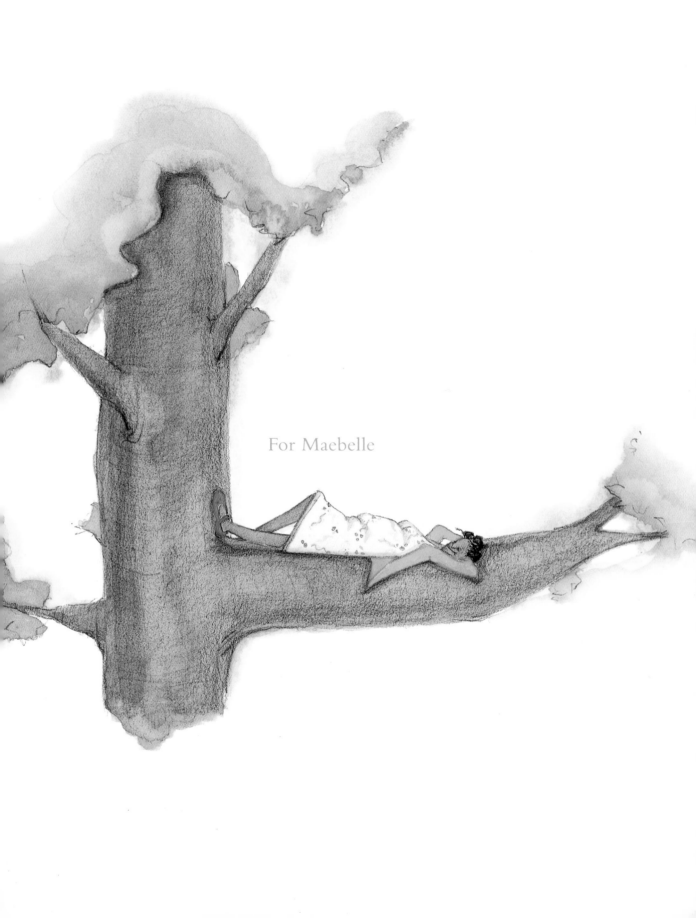

For Maebelle

Maebelle was one hundred and eight years old and had spent the last eight living happily among the treetops. A fascination with birds had inspired her to build her own treehouse.

Maebelle made hats and sold them to a little shop in town. For the moment, she had put aside her work and was adding the finishing touch to a special project—her entry in the town's annual hat contest.

The hat was finished, and Maebelle was very, very
pleased. Out on her porch she relaxed.

From up above, she heard a chorus of good-byes. Winter
was on its way, and her neighbors were heading south.

There was a knock at her door. It was young Binkle.

"Maebelle, may I borrow a suitcase?" he asked. "I promise to return it in a few months."

"Now, pum'kin, why on earth do you want a suitcase?"

"I can't leave home without my belongings!"

Maebelle watched Binkle fill the suitcase. In went an oak branch forked at one end, some round rocks, and a small pile of dirt. He added a few daisies and gardenias and an armful of elm leaves. Then he tucked in his nest.

"I'm ready to fly south now, Maebelle." Binkle sighed sadly. "I sure will miss you."

"Cheer up, Binkle. You'll be back. Besides, traveling is fun."

Binkle gave Maebelle a big hug.

Over and over again, he tried to fly up and away.

But each time he landed flat on his back.

"You silly bird," said Maebelle. "You'd be a lot better off
if you'd let go of this load."

"Leave it behind? Absolutely not! I couldn't!"

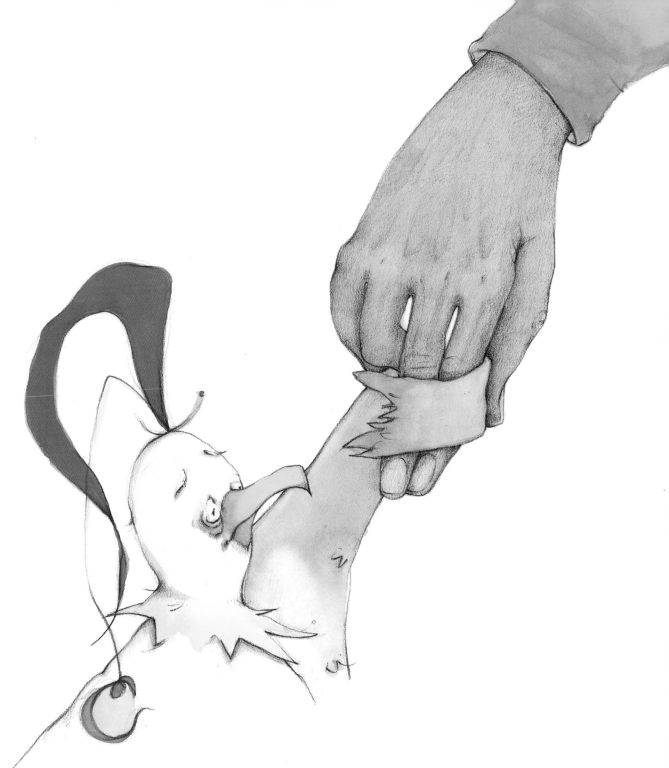

"Hmmm. . . . Well, at least come inside and rest while I
work on my project," she said.

"What project?"

"I'm making a hat for the big contest tomorrow. But I can't find certain things I need."

"Like what?"

"For one, a handsome oak branch forked at one end."

Maebelle sighed. "I just don't know what to do."
"Maybe I can help," said Binkle. And away he flew.

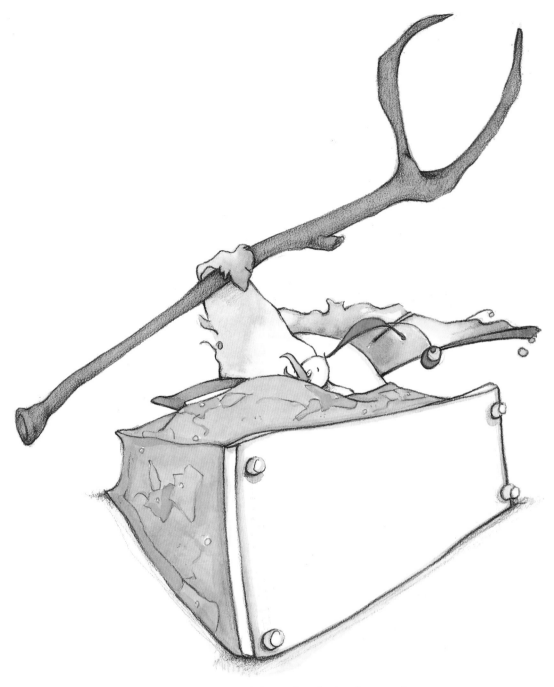

Binkle returned. "I couldn't find the branch you described. But"—he reached into the suitcase—"will this do?"

"Perfect!" said Maebelle. "Now, if only I could find some shiny, round rocks and rich, brown earth."

"I happen to have some inside this suitcase," Binkle exclaimed, surprised.

"Oh, Binkle! Thank you!"

"Is there something else I can help you with?"

"I need some daisies and gardenias."

"No problem. Be back in a flash."

"And if you find some elm leaves, I'd greatly appreciate them," Maebelle called out.

"Right!"

Binkle returned almost immediately, his wings empty.
"Couldn't you find the flowers?" Maebelle asked.
"Well," said Binkle, "it seems I have just what you need in the suitcase. You can return everything to me after the contest, and then I'll be on my way."
"Binkle, you've been such a help. Now I can begin."

Binkle watched in awe while Maebelle created the hat. When she had finished, he cried, "Bravo! A true masterpiece!"

"But something's missing," Maebelle said.

"May I make a suggestion?" Binkle asked timidly.

Carefully he pulled his nest out of the suitcase and placed it at the top of the hat. Inside the nest lay the shell from which Binkle had been born.

In silence, Maebelle and Binkle stared proudly at the sight before them.

"How will I wear it?" whispered Maebelle.

"Easy," said Binkle. "I've got the answer right here."

The next day arrived, and what a happy day it was. Maebelle did not win the contest. However, the judges invented a new prize for Maebelle and Binkle. They received an award for the most original hat.

Furthermore, the hat was put on permanent display at the
town museum, to be preserved and honored always.

As Maebelle and Binkle headed back to the treehouse, a cool gust of air swept by. Binkle shuddered. "I can't take this cold. I really must move on."

"I know, and I'll miss you," Maebelle said.

"I'll miss you, too, Maebelle. But I'll be back."

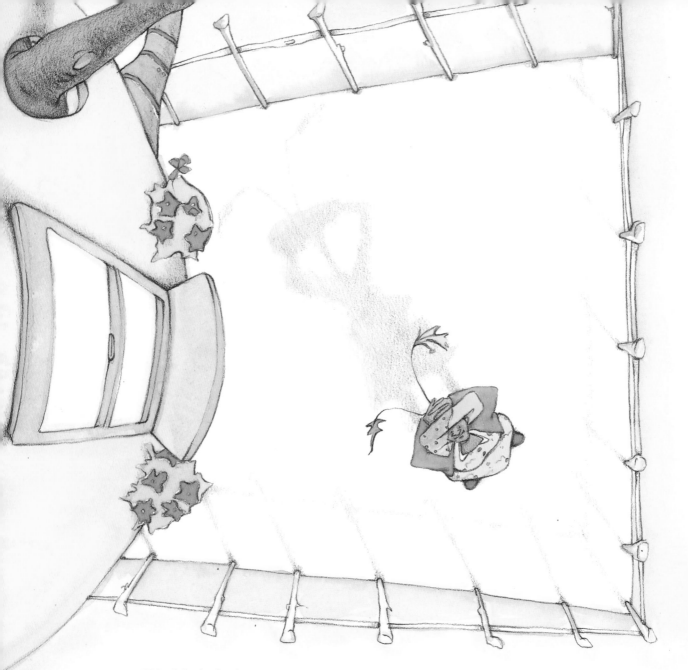

Binkle left that afternoon. Maebelle knew he was taking a detour to get one last proud look through the museum window.

Once alone, Maebelle placed the hat she had originally made for the contest on her head. "Maybe next year," she said softly.